TREASURE IS

by ROBERT LOUIS STEVENSON

#5 # Adventure at Sea

WITHDRAWN

Adapted by Catherine Nichols

Illustrated by Sally Wern Comport

STERLING

New York / London

www.sterlingpublishing.com/kids

STERLING and the distinctive Sterling logo are
registered trademarks of Sterling Publishing Co., Inc.

Library of Congress Cataloging-in-Publication Data Available

Lot #: 10 9 8 7 6 5 4 3 2 1
02/10
Published by Sterling Publishing Co., Inc.
387 Park Avenue South, New York, NY 10016
© 2010 by Sterling Publishing Co., Inc.
Illustrations © 2010 by Sally Wern Comport
Distributed in Canada by Sterling Publishing
c/o Canadian Manda Group, 165 Dufferin Street
Toronto, Ontario, Canada M6K 3H6
Distributed in the United Kingdom by GMC Distribution Services
Castle Place, 166 High Street, Lewes, East Sussex, England BN7 1XU
Distributed in Australia by Capricorn Link (Australia) Pty. Ltd.
P.O. Box 704, Windsor, NSW 2756, Australia

Sterling ISBN 978-1-4027-6751-7

For information about custom editions, special sales, premium and
corporate purchases, please contact Sterling Special Sales
Department at 800-805-5489 or specialsales@sterlingpublishing.com.

Contents

A Dangerous Plan

Jim Hawkins was trapped.

He and his friends had a map

that led to buried treasure.

But pirates were attacking their fort

on Treasure Island.

The pirates wanted the treasure too.

The map was safe in the fort,
and so were Jim and his friends.
But for how long?

The pirates left the fort.
Some stayed on the island.
Others stole the ship that
Jim and his friends had sailed
to Treasure Island.

If the pirates got away,

Jim and his friends would be left behind.

Jim needed a plan—and fast!

What if Jim could somehow
get to the ship?
He could cut the rope
tied to the anchor.
The ship would drift to the shore
and get stuck in the sand.
Then the pirates couldn't sail away.

The plan was dangerous.

Jim's friends didn't want him to go.

Jim made up his mind.

He would go anyway.

He grabbed some snacks
for his dinner.

Then he took a sharp knife
to cut the rope.

Jim waited
until his friends were busy.
Then he slipped
out of the fort.
He ran into the woods.
He was free!

Swept Away

Jim walked down to the beach.
The ship looked
almost the same,
only now a pirate flag
was tied to its mast.
Seeing it made Jim angry.
How he wished
he could tear the flag down!

Jim knew where
he could find a boat.
A friend had hidden one
near a white rock.
Jim went to the spot.
There was the boat!
It was as round as a cup
and very small.

As soon as it grew dark,

Jim climbed into the boat.

He could just fit inside.

The night was foggy.

No one would see him.

At first, it was hard
to row the round boat,
but with practice,
he was able to steer it.
Soon he was beside
the tall ship.

A thick rope kept the ship
from sailing.
Jim began to cut the rope.
It was slow work.
Finally only a few strands
were left.

Jim slashed at the last pieces of rope.
As the rope dropped into the water,
the ship started to drift away.
Jim hoped it would get stuck in
the sand.

Just at that moment a strong wind blew.

The ship went faster.

So did Jim's boat.

Waves tossed it this way and that.

Jim rowed and rowed.

If he couldn't get back to shore,

he would be swept out to sea!

Last Chance

All night Jim's boat went
round and round Treasure Island.
No matter how hard he rowed,
he couldn't get close to shore.
Ahead of him, the big ship drifted too.
No one was steering it.
The pirates must have jumped
off the ship in the storm.

Finally it was morning.

Jim was tired and thirsty.

His arms hurt from rowing.

He couldn't go on

for much longer.

What would happen to him?

Somehow he had to get
onto the ship.
Maybe he could steer it
back to shore.
Then his friends would have
their ship back.

Suddenly the wind changed direction.

The big ship began to spin in circles.

When the wind stopped,

Jim saw that

the ship had turned around.

Now it was pointed at Jim.

And it was racing

toward his little boat!

A long pole stuck out
from the ship.
As it passed over him,
Jim reached up.
He grabbed it
with both hands.
He held on tight.

He was just in time.

The ship crashed into the boat.

The small boat sank without a trace.

Captain of the Ship

Jim clung to the pole.

His feet dangled in the air.

Carefully, he pulled himself up.

At last his feet touched the deck.

Jim searched the ship
for pirates.
He was alone.
Suddenly he knew
what he had to do.

Jim climbed to the top of the mast.

He grabbed the pirate flag

and tore it down.

It fell on the deck below.

"I am captain of this ship," he shouted.

Jim made a new plan.
He would steer the ship
to a part of the island
where no one could find it.
Later he and his friends
would sail off and leave
the pirates behind.

In the distance
Jim saw the fort.
He couldn't wait
to see his friends again.
He had so much to tell them
about his adventure at sea!